For Denise and Klaus

First published in Great Britain in 1994
by Andersen Press Limited

ISBN 0-590-37643-8

12 11 10 9 8 7 6 5 4 3 2 1

8 9/9 0 1 2 3/0

14

Printed in the U.S.A.

First Scholastic printing, September 1998

Suddenly!

Words and Pictures by
Colin McNaughton

SCHOLASTIC INC.
New York Toronto London Auckland Sydney

Preston was walking home from school one day when

suddenly!

Preston remembered
his mother had asked
him to go to the store.

Preston was doing
the shopping when

suddenly!

He dashed out of the store! He remembered he had left the grocery money in his school desk.

Ah, *there it is.*

Preston got the money
from his desk and
was coming out of
the school when

suddenly!

Preston decided to use the back door.

On his way back to the store
Preston stopped by the park
to play when

suddenly!

Billy the bully
shoved past him and
went down the slide!

Preston climbed down
from the slide and went
on to do the shopping.
He was just coming out
of the store when

suddenly!

Mr. Plimp the storekeeper
called Preston back to
say he had forgotten
his change.

Silly me!

At last Preston arrived home. " Mom," he said, "I've had the strangest feeling that someone has been following me."

Suddenly!

Preston's mother turned around and gave him an enormous
hug!